This edition first published in 2004 by
Cat's Whiskers
96 Leonard Street
London EC2A 4XD

ISBN 1 903012 71 6 (hbk)
ISBN 1 903012 72 4 (pbk)

Originally published in Belgium by Uitgeverij Clavis
Amsterdam-Hasselt 2003
Text and illustrations copyright © Uitgeverij Clavis
Amsterdam-Hasselt 2003
English text copyright © Cat's Whiskers 2004

A CIP catalogue record for this book is available from the
British Library

Printed in Italy

Guido Van Genechten

Flop-Ear
and his Friends

CAT'S Whiskers

It was time to play!
Flop-Ear ran through the trees
to the clearing in the forest.

All the rabbits were there,
playing different games.

The white rabbits were
playing balance-the-carrot.

Flop-Ear was good at this;
his carrot didn't fall off even
when he was standing on one leg.

The grey rabbits were playing
fly-a-kite. What fun,
thought Flop-Ear — but be
careful when you land!

The brown rabbits were playing
leapfrog. Up and over!
Flop-Ear loved it.

The black rabbits were playing trains.
"Come along, climb aboard!" they shouted.
Flop-Ear was the driver.

All afternoon, different groups of rabbits
played their favourite games.
But one rabbit stood on his own,
just watching. He was new to the forest,
and looked different. He was spotty.

Flop-Ear went over to him.
"Hello, I'm Flop-Ear.
What's your name?"
"Patch," said the spotty rabbit.
"Why don't you come and play?"
asked Flop-Ear.
Patch replied shyly, "I don't
know any of the games."
Flop-Ear took him by the
paw. "Come with me and
I'll show you."

Flop-Ear showed Patch how to
balance a carrot on his head.

Patch tried and soon he could do
it really well, even on one leg.

Patch said, "Let's play somersault-thunderbolt."

"What's that?" asked Flop-Ear.
"Well, you do three somersaults very fast,
then you splutter PPRRRT on your paw
with your tongue." Flop-Ear laughed.
That sounded like fun!

The other rabbits came over.
"Who's your new friend?" they asked.
The other rabbits thought Patch looked funny.
"Patchy paws, patchy paws!" they teased him.

"Stop it!" shouted Flop-Ear. "Patch knows a really good game. It's called carrot-kite-leapfrog-train-somersault-thunderbolt."

Flop-Ear had made up a completely NEW GAME!

"You balance a carrot, fly a kite, leapfrog, make a train, somersault three times — and then the very best part is the thunderbolt, just like this PPRRRT," said Flop-Ear.

The rabbits thought this was the best
game ever. And soon they were all
playing it – ALL TOGETHER!